ROBOT REPAIRS

(T̲echnology)

Written by
Jonathan Litton

Illustrated by
Magalí Mansilla

Max and Suzy were helping to clear up
Miss Eureka's workshop.

"Hey Suzy, look!" said Max.
"It's Robbie, the old robot from school!"

"I wonder if he still works?" said Suzy. "There are
batteries in the box. Shall we put them in and see?"

Max reached out for the batteries, but...

3

DISASTER!

Max tripped over the broom and fell, smashing
Robbie the robot to smithereens!

4

"Oops!" giggled Suzy. "Are you OK, Max?"

Max sat up, surrounded by robot parts.
There were arms and legs, cogs and
wheels, springs and switches everywhere!

"I'm fine," laughed Max. "We're going to
need more than batteries now, Suzy."

"Robbie used to walk and talk, a bit like you and me. Do you think we can put him back together again, Suzy?" Max asked.

"Of course, Max, we'll work it out," replied Suzy. "Look! I've found some motors and a circuit."

"There are two big motors and two small ones. They must power the arms and legs. I wonder which ones are which? Do legs or arms need the most power?" she asked.

Max practiced a karate chop,
and said, "My arms are
really powerful!"

Then Suzy bent her knees
and used her legs to leap
into the air. "Legs are even more
powerful than arms!" she said.

"You're right," said Max, "The large motors must power the legs and the smaller ones must be for the arms."

Suzy and Max attached the arms and legs.
Robbie was starting to look like a robot again!

"I've slotted the circuit inside his head.
Now let's try to attach it," said Max.

They pushed and pushed as hard as they could, but the head would not go on.

"Let's hit it with a hammer!" suggested Suzy.

"Did I hear the word *hammer*?" said Miss Eureka, appearing suddenly.
Max and Suzy looked surprised.

"You're rebuilding Robbie, the robot I see!" said Miss Eureka.
"Do you need my help?"

"Yes please," said Suzy. "We're having problems with his head."

"Take a look at this jar," said Miss Eureka. "It has grooves around the neck, just like Robbie. How do we put the lid on the jar?" she asked.

"YOU TWIST IT!" said Max and Suzy together.

"Let's see if we can twist Robbie's head back on," said Max and Suzy. They gently lifted the head and slowly twisted it back into place.

WELL DONE!

"Now we need to do some more twisting and turning to attach the ears," said Miss Eureka.

screwdriver

hammer

wrench

"Which tool shall we use?
The screwdriver, hammer, or wrench?"

15

Max chose the wrench. He tightened it around the ears and gently turned, so that the ears screwed into place.

"I'm glad you didn't use the hammer," laughed Miss Eureka. "You would have smashed the ears to pieces. And a screwdriver can't turn that big bolt."

Robbie was almost ready,
but something was still missing ...

"Is it time to put the battery in?" asked Suzy.

"Yes, almost done!" said Miss Eureka.

"Open up the chest and you'll see

where it goes."

"We have to match the plus and minus signs on the battery to the insides," said Max.

"Here we go," said Suzy, lining up the battery.

They placed the battery inside Robbie's chest,
closed the lid, and pressed the ON button.
He leaped up and started dancing!

I'M ROBBIE THE ROBOT!

"We did it!" shouted Suzy and Max,
doing their best robot dance.
"Well done!" said Miss Eureka.
"You're real technology whiz kids!"

The technology behind the story

Let's look at the problems Suzy and Max faced in the story. Turn to the page numbers for help, or find the answers on the next page.

p.9

p.8

Problem solving

Suzy and Max decide to rebuild the robot. First, they plan what they need to do.

In what way are the motors different?

How did Max and Suzy figure out what job each motor did?

Your turn

Suzy and Max faced a few problems when building Robbie. They asked questions and thought of solutions. Have you ever faced a problem? What was it? How did you fix it?

p.14
p.15

Using tools

It's important to use the right tool for the right job.

How did Max attach Robbie's head? What tool did he use for the ears?

Can you name these tools?

Your turn

Choosing the right tools will help you complete your task. What do you use a hammer for? How is this different from using a wrench or a screwdriver?

p.19

Providing power

A battery stores energy and can supply electricity to bulbs and motors.

How did Suzy make Robbie walk and talk?

Your turn

Many things in your home are powered by electricity which comes through plugs from the main electrical grid. Which items use batteries and which items need grid power?

Answers

If you need help finding the answers, try reading the page again.

Problem solving: Two of the motors are large and two are small. Suzy and Max figured out that the large motors power the legs, and the small motors power the arms.

Using tools: Max twisted Robbie's head into the neck. Then he used the wrench to attach the ears.

Tools: screwdriver, hammer, and wrench.

Providing power: Suzy placed the battery into Robbie's chest and switched him on.

Quarto is the authority on a wide range of topics.

Quarto educates, entertains and enriches the lives of our readers—enthusiasts and lovers of hands-on living.

www.quartoknows.com

Author: Jonathan Litton
Illustrator: Magalí Mansilla
Consultant: Ed Walsh
Editors: Jacqueline McCann, Carly Madden, Ellie Brough
Designer: Sarah Chapman-Suire

© 2018 Quarto Publishing plc

First published in 2018 by QEB Publishing,
An imprint of The Quarto Group
6 Orchard Road, Suite 100
Lake Forest, CA 92630
T: +1 949 380 7510
F: +1 949 380 7575
www.QuartoKnows.com

MIX
Paper from responsible sources
FSC® C104723

A CIP record for this book is available from the Library of Congress.

ISBN 978 1 78603 279 9

9 8 7 6 5 4 3 2 1

Manufactured in Dongguan, China
TL052018

Find out more...

Here are links to websites where you will find more information on technology, including electricity.

PBS Kids
www.pbskids.org/cyberchase/find-it/science-and-engineering/

Ecosystems for Kids
www.ecosystemforkids.com/electricity-and-magnetism.html

CHILDREN SHOULD BE SUPERVISED WHEN USING THE INTERNET, PARTICULARLY WHEN USING AN UNFAMILIAR WEBSITE FOR THE FIRST TIME. THE PUBLISHERS AND AUTHOR CANNOT BE HELD RESPONSIBLE FOR THE CONTENT OF THE WEBSITES REFERRED TO IN THIS BOOK.